Finding Christmas

A Mouse in Search of Christmas

Keeping the Art of Storytelling Alive

by

Dr. Carrie Wachsmann

Finding Christmas

Copyright © 2018 Dr. Carrie Wachsmann

Cover design, digital artwork, drawings - Dr. Carrie Wachsmann

Editor - Dr. Win Wachsmann

Mice Photographer - Bruce McCaughey

Cover background forest and snow image - Public Domain

Visualhunt.com - Creative Commons images

Public Domain/fair use images

Published by

HeartBeat Productions Inc.

Box 633, Abbotsford, BC, Canada V2T 6Z8

email: info@heartbeat1.com

tel: 604.852.3769

ISBN 978-1-895112-61-0   (paperback)

Printed in the US

HeartBeat PRODUCTIONS INC.

Finding Christmas

Characters

Bella - city mouse - lives in the woodpile at 33406 Walnut Lane in Abbyville

Marko - country mouse - lives in Farmer Brown's field in the country 2 miles from Abbyville

Brutus - lonely, scruffy goat lives in the forest with his master, befriends Marko

Mr. & Mrs. Waxmann - own enchanting home on 33406 Walnut Lane

Sabrina & Amy - Mr. & Mrs. Waxmann's grandchildren who befriend Bella and Marko

Karl and Wendy - own Karl's Meat Market and where country and city mice get their special cheese

Baby Jesus - the baby in the straw

24 Guardian Mouse Angels - can be found in the most unexpected places

Can you find them all?

Dedicated
to the baby in the straw

Thank You

to daughter, **Minde**, whose creative ideas lead to adding the endearing, guarding-mice characters.

to grandson, **Mark**, who loves adventure and furry little creatures... like his hamster, Sweetie and their curious, elusive country mouse who's taken residence in their kitchen.

to my husband, **Win**, whose editing skills give my storytelling that extra bit of specialness. Thank you again.

to **Bruce McCaughey**, whose photographs make Marko and Bella come alive in a most excellent way.

Background Story

Story sets and mice slide photos were originally created in 1981 for a church, Christmas slide-story presentation. In 2017, I updated my little mouse Christmas story. I scanned the slides, reworked the images with Photoshop and having lost the original script, I rewrote the story.

Finding Christmas was originally titled, *Where's Christmas?*.

nce upon a time...

a bright-eyed and adventurous city mouse named Bella lived in the little city of Abbyville. She lived alone in her modest but charming habitat at 33406 Walnut Lane, her cozy abode neatly hidden and nestled amongst the firewood beside Mr. and Mrs. Waxmann's woodshed.

On occasion, Bella and Mr. Waxmann had a chance to meet, and from the tone of his voice and the manner in which he spoke, Bella felt confident Mr. Waxmann was quite safe.

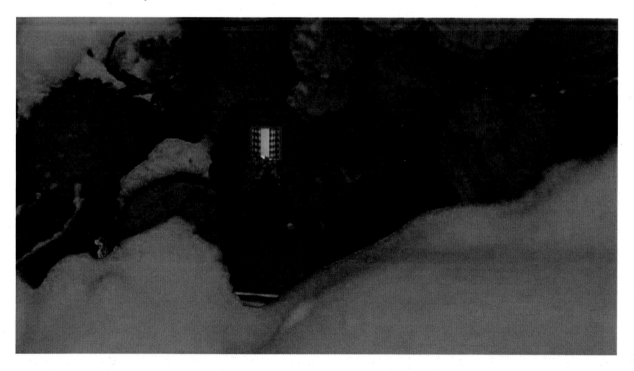

Mrs. Waxmann was another matter altogether. Once, when they happened to cross paths, Mrs. Waxmann let out a rather chilling screech, and although Bella let out a squeal of her own, she found it quite humorous to see the sweet-faced, rotund woman run back into the house faster than a fox on a goose chase. Since then, Mrs. Waxmann rarely visited the woodshed. Bella felt quite at home at 33406 Walnut Lane.

A few months prior, feeling all grown up and brave, Bella had moved out of her parent's home. Her parents lived just a block down the street and she could visit any time she liked. Walnut Lane was a quiet lane on the outskirts of town and that's the way Bella and her family liked it. If at all possible, Bella avoided the downtown area which bustled with activity from early morning to late at night.

The odd time, Bella would make a treck into town in the evening hours for a nice big chunk of Swiss cheese, one she could find at the popular Karl's Dutch Meat Market some 15 minutes from her home.

It took a bit of sneaking about to get that special piece of cheese, but for Bella the effort was worth it. She found lots of wonderful smelling cheeses in the garbage can just beside the cheese cutting counter. Up to this time, Bella had gone unnoticed, although the last time she made a cheese run, she overheard Mr. Karl telling his wife Wendy he thought "...we just might have a mouse problem!"

Did that deter Bella? Not in the least. She determined she would just have to be more careful.

Although Bella was very happy with her life, she had one wish. She wished for a friend. Someone with whom she could share her adventures and someone to have her back when trouble happened—if trouble were to happen.

Bella's wish was soon to come true...

8

Marko, a handsome, strong and brave country mouse would soon appear. He lived in a thriving mouse community in farmer Brown's 6-acre cow pasture, at the edge of the forest. Farmer Brown, his wife, their 47 Holstein cows, 2 German Shepherd dogs and 3 cats lived 2 miles and 3 1/2 barn lengths from Abbyville; so "they" said.

In the recent past, a few of the country mice community (whom we will call "they") had ventured to Abbyville, wanting to see for themselves what life was like in the city. On their return, some told stories how exciting and fun the city was. Others said it was dangerous and frightening, and they were only too happy to be back home in the safety of their quiet countryside. At least here they knew what dangers to expect.

One of the stories that floated around the country-mouse village was what Abbyvillers called "Christmas." None of the mice knew what Christmas was.

"They" said, if one wanted to find out, one would have to visit the city during the coldest time of the year—in the dead of winter.

One thing "they" did know, was Christmas had something to do with peace on earth and goodwill toward men, and that it was a very merry time of the year.

Peace on earth, goodwill to men? Merry time of the year? What is that all about? Marko wondered.

Since he had not been one of the brave ones who went to the city, Marko's curiosity about "Merry Christmas" and the city grew.

The dead of winter came. The country-mouse community was safe and warm in their cozy habitats and many burrows beneath the frozen snow-covered field. They had plenty of supplies to keep them fat and content throughout the long winter months. Until springtime, any ventures into the world above would be few and far between.

Marko was restless. If he were going to find out what "Christmas" was about, he would have to make that trip into the city—and he would have to make it now.

"It's now or never," Marko determined. He dressed warmly, filled his pockets with nuts, slipped on his earmuffs, and said a cheery goodbye to his family and friends. Everyone wished him well.

"We'll say a prayer for you every day," his mother said.

"Trust your God-given instincts and you'll do just fine," his father added.

"Bring us back some Swiss cheese," his friends implored.

Marko smiled. "Sure guys. Swiss cheese it is. Don't worry, Mama, Papa, I'll be back before you know it." And he bravely went on his way.

What a beautiful morning it was. "I really should get out more in winter," Marko muttered to himself. "What fun we could have in this snow."

And then he was off. Marko's little feet fairly flew over the endless white mountains of snow.

Background Forest with Snow/ public domain

At times, where the snow was extra soft, Marko resorted to tunneling, but undaunted, he traveled along at a good and constant pace.

Marko knew that a dark-colored rodent scurrying across a blanket of white snow was easy prey for a sharp-eyed hawk or monstrous eagle-dragon. And then, there was the red fox, or even worse, the camouflaged silver fox. They could pounce out of nowhere, and Marko knew what that would mean... Oh, he didn't want to think about what that would mean. So he kept his cool and he diligently watched for moving shadows.

And then that dreaded shadow...

Marko dived into the snowbank, tunneling as fast as he could until he bumped into a log. Finding a split, he squeezed into it and stayed there until he stopped trembling... and he had eaten his stash of energy nuts in his pocket.

Finally, he cautiously returned to the surface. Seeing no predators, he continued on his way.

He would have to be extra vigilant. Not more than fifteen minutes had passed when Marko noticed a Snowy Owl, perched on a tree stump, mere meters away. Marko knew snowy owls were not nocturnal, like most owls, who only hunt at night. Snowy owls are diurnal and can hunt and be active both day and night.

"He hasn't spotted me. Maybe I can slip past him." But the next second the Snowy Owl swiveled his head 160 degrees and locked its gaze on Marko.

Photo of Eagle - gokulmyphoto on Visualhunt.com/CC BY-SA
Background Forest and Snow/ public domain

13

"Oh, boy! Am I in trouble!"

Marko did not waste a moment... He scrambled under a bushy shrub and sat perfectly still. With a big swoosh, the owl made a graceful landing right next to where Marko was hiding. Marko could see the creature's large talons just inches from him.

photo of owl-synspectrum on Visual Hunt/CC BY
Background Forest with Snow/public domain

The owl hopped about for a minute and then, realizing his dinner had eluded him, flapped his strong wings, and flew out of sight.

"Whew, another close one," Marko muttered as he once again carefully checked his surroundings. Bravely, he scurried along.

Marko was not surprised when, several hours later he encountered a fox. Thankfully, it was a red fox and not the hard-to-see silver fox.

Fox/visual hunt/public domain

A fox has very keen ears. Whether silver or red, a fox can hear a mouse while the mouse is moving under a foot or two of soft snow. First, the fox listens to where the mouse might be. Then, with amazing accuracy, he jumps up into the air and dives head first into the snow. The fox rises out of the snow with his prey in his mouth.

Marko had just enough time to hide behind a giant pine cone and dig into the snow far enough to be covered. He remembered what his father had told him. "If you've no other option, play dead. Don't panic, keep your heartbeat down, and do not move a muscle. Chances are, you'll save yourself."

Marko could sense the fox coming closer and closer...

He could feel the pads of the wily fox's feet hit the snow. One, two, three, four. Closer and closer they came. It took every bit of willpower for Marko not to tunnel and run. He held his breath, listened to his heartbeat, and prayed a prayer.

Marko's strategy worked. The fox moved on. Marko had crossed paths with a fox, and won.

As one can imagine, Marko was grateful the rest of the journey was uneventful; except for a couple of barking dogs, who posed no threat whatsoever, and one scruffy billy-goat who just wanted someone to play with.

"I've been wishing for someone to play with me, and here you are," the sorry-looking goat bleated.

"Oh, I don't have time for play," Marko responded. "I'm on a very important journey..." But when he noticed the longing look on the billy-goat's face— he hesitated...

He looks kinda lonely. How can I not take time to play with a goat as friendly as this one? "Even so, I think I can take a few minutes to romp with you. Might I suggest a game of hide and seek?"

"Ha, you are a sly one. You, of course, have the advantage, being so small and all. Why you could hide forever in that woodpile. And what can I do about it?"

"I hadn't thought of that. What if I agree to keep it fair. I won't hide in the woodpile."

The goat butted his head into the nearest log in agreement, then did a delighted skip straight up into the air. The next second, the game was on.

Amidst all the fun and frolic, Marko learned his new friend's name was Brutus. Brutus told him he had a master, whose rustic cabin they could see nestled among the trees nearby.

"Master is very good to me, but he's too old to play. I watch out for him. I even chased off a bear one day. He was very proud of me."

"I'm sure he was. You're a pretty brave goat, and your master is lucky to have you. And I am lucky to have met you."

Brutus shared his lunch of cabbage and carrots, and they even took a 15 minute nap.

Refreshed, Marko said, "It's time for me to be on my way. I've had so much fun and thanks for sharing your lunch."

"If you must go... perhaps you can drop by again sometime?"

"How about I stop by on my way back home?"

"I'll watch for you. And you can stay awhile. Master always has cheese and apples. I'll save you some."

"It's a plan then," Marko said, "Two of my favorite treats. I'll see you soon, my friend." And he scampered off.

"Keep safe," Brutus bleated. "I'll be watching... Don't forget now..."

Marko stopped and waved one last goodbye. "Not to worry, I won't forget. How could I?" He shouted back.

I never thought I would ever have a goat for a friend. That just goes to show you, never judge a goat by his scruffiness.

The shadows began to lengthen as Marko neared his destination. In the distance he could see the city glowing in the darkness, nestled among snow-tipped evergreens and hoarfrost-laden deciduous branches.

A light snow began to fall as Marko entered the outskirts of Abbyville. He stopped to catch his breath. *Now where to go?* He decided the more trees, the better he was protected, so he scurried down a street called Maplewood.

20

Here the homes were tall and nestled close to each other. Every home on the street had a myriad of colorful lights attached to it. Even many of the trees had lights entwined among the branches.

He turned onto a lane called Walnut. He liked this street much better. It had a peaceful and quiet feel about it.

Marko had no idea what to do next, but he knew, like his Papa said, he could trust his instincts to guide him.

He stopped at a house where welcome-candles flickered and glowed in every window.

That is the most enchanted human habitat I've ever seen...

Then something caught his eye. Something looking just like him scurried across the front porch, jumped onto the ground and scurried on some more, disappearing into the backyard.

"A mouse, another mouse!" Marko declared excitedly. He raced to the porch and followed the fresh tracks. The tracks led him to an inviting little guest cottage; a woodshed attached to it. Next to the cottage, which was also covered in colorful, sparkling lights, he saw a great pile of logs.

The tracks he was following became mixed with other imprints, not all belonging to mice. Some crisscrossed here and there and most everywhere.

Where would a city mouse make their habitat? Marko pondered. *The log pile, for one.* Sure enough, he found a door. Light beamed through a small window, with a sprig of ruby-red berries hung beneath it.

This looks welcoming. Marko took a deep breath, stepped up to the door and knocked.

23

I hope they're friendly, was his last thought before the door opened.

"Oh, good. You're not that crazy nut, Wilford."

Marko was momentarily startled. A pretty mouse with attractive brown eyes was talking.

"Wilford?" No..nooo...I'm not...Who's Wilford?

"A most bothersome squirrel who likes to play tricks on me; steal my nuts and such."

"I'm not a squirrel." Marko laughed.

"I can see that. So, who are you then?"

"Marko. I am a country mouse come to visit the city."

"A country mouse, you say? I've never met a country mouse before. Well, you don't look all that different and you look quite harmless. My name is Bella."

"Nice to meet you, Bella."

"Would you like to come in then?"

"I'd like that. I'm tuckered right out."

"Tuckered out?"

"That's just what we call tired. A country saying, you know."

"Well then, what if I make you a hot drink to go along with my fresh-baked walnut-date cookies. I was about to have some. That should help you get untuckered."

They both laughed. "Good one," Marko said.

"I thought so too," Bella answered.

She's a bit of a cheeky one, Marko thought. *I like her.*

"I don't ever get visitors. I was just thinking how it would be nice to have a visitor, and here you are," Bella said. "I've only lived here for a short while, and don't seem to have any mouse neighbors."

She certainly knows how to make someone feel welcome. Gratefully, Marko stepped into the warm and cozy kitchen. *Hot drink and walnut-date cookies!*

"I'm happy to be your first visitor and I will gladly accept those cookies. I ate my stash of nuts hours ago while hiding from an eagle-dragon."

"Eagle-dragon! You were chased by an eagle-dragon?"

"Yah. But, it was nothin' really; we're kinda use to that sort of thing in the country."

"You are? Even so, that must have been scary."

"Yes, it was very scary."

"Why do you want to visit the city?" Bella asked. "You must have a very important reason to travel such a distance and risk your life."

"Our mouse community heard about something the people in Abbyville call 'Christmas.' Last year, a few of our clan; the braver, more mature ones of course, ventured into the city on a special cheese run."

"When they got back, and after everyone had feasted on some of the most delicious cheese ever, they told how everyone in the city was preparing for 'Christmas.'"

"They couldn't tell us what 'Christmas' was all about, only that 'it was a very merry time of the year, and it had something to do with 'peace on earth and goodwill to men.' That got me curious; so curious I could not stop thinking about it. So here I am."

"Christmas? You country folk don't know about Christmas. You've come to the right place. I know exactly where to take you. But first you need to sit down, relax and have some cookies. You'll need to be rested and fed up before I take you to Christmas. What do you say?"

"I say that would be awesome."

Marko and Bella chatted like long lost friends as they nibbled on Bella's cookies and sipped on creamy, steamed milk. They discovered that, although they came from totally different worlds, they were very much alike. They liked the same foods and they liked new adventures. They had some of the same enemies, and they shared the same instincts.

"This is the time of night downtown Abbyville will be bustling with all kinds of activity," Bella said. "It's the best time to discover Christmas. Be warned, you will find it kind of scary at times, with all the people rushing here and there, and the cars and busses and such, but if you stick close to me, we'll be OK."

"Don't YOU find that scary?"

"Oh, I do, but I've been well taught in city-mouse street-safety and awareness. I've done this numerous of times."

"We're in for some excitement then?"

"You can count on that."

Marko slipped on his earmuffs and drained the last drops from his glass.

Bella put on her coat, draped her scarf around her neck and slipped on a pair of matching earmuffs.

"Are you ready?" Bella asked.

"Of course," Marko answered.

"Good, then let's do this."

Together they stepped into the night. All was calm, the streets were bright.

But as they got closer to main street, the traffic became noisier and disconcertingly congested. Lights flashed everywhere. Vehicles swished past them. Horns blasted and sirens blared.

"We almost there?" Marko shouted after a speeding car splattered them with dirty, gobs of slush. He helped Bella wipe off the slush from her petticoat.

"You'll be pleased to know, we're through the worst of it. We've got one more busy street to maneuver and then we'll just have shopper's feet to navigate. OK, let's make a run for it."

They ran. A few slips and slides, another messy snow wash, and they made it safely to the sidewalk.

Marko was relieved the shoppers were much too captivated by whatever it was in the store windows to notice them.

Dmitryelj/photo on flickr/visual hunt/CC

"That's what I'm counting on. And what's in those windows is the reason why we're here. They'll tell you plenty about Christmas. They're called Christmas window displays." Bella explained.

"Look, this one's almost like the country. I like this window," Marko exclaimed. He said he found the Feed and Seed store and workhorse display comforting.

They passed dancing bears, Christmas trees covered with shiny baubles, and fancy wrapped boxes tucked underneath the pine branches.

Dancing Dolls in window display/ public domain

Bella pointed to the next window. "I like this one. The house where I grew up and my parents live, the family has a little girl who looks just like that one right there, in the green coat. When Cindy... that's her name, Cindy. When Cindy had tea time with her doll friends, she'd leave me delicious treats."

"Sometimes mice and folks can be friends, I've heard."

"Oh yes, it's true. We had many good times together."

"What are they singing?" Marko asked.

"They're singing songs about Christmas. They're called Carolers. Sometimes for real, people sing on the street. Or sometimes a group of carolers walk around to people's homes and sing at their windows. It's quite pleasant really."

"Christmas Carolers sound cool. I hope we get to hear them sing."

Bella and Marko scampered on to the next window. "Ah, this one says it all," Marko said. "So many clocks. Everyone's in such a rush to get somewhere. Everybody's on the clock here in Abbyville."

"Humans have so much to prepare before Christmas day. Christmas season is all month long, and then there's the one special Christmas Day."

"I think people fuss and worry too much. They should just enjoy the time."

santuous clocks window display/ public domain

"Some people get so worked up during Christmas month they cry about little things or get sore at nothing," Bella added.

"That's true in the country too. About always being busy. Farmer Brown is up at 4:30 in the morning and doesn't stop till night. And Mrs. Brown, if she isn't washing clothes, she's baking bread, or helping with the cows. Being a human must be quite exhausting."

Bella laughed. "It must be. I'm glad I'm a mouse."

The next window they came to had a little boy and girl trying to put a letter into an overstuffed mailbox. Marko said, "This one's interesting."

"It's fun and friendly," Bella said.

"The mailbox is overflowing...and it looks like all of those letters are addressed to someone called Santa Claus. I wonder who this Santa Claus is. He must be important for so many people to be mailing letters to him."

"Santa Claus seems to be very important at Christmas," Bella answered. "They say he flies through the sky and drops off gifts for every child on Christmas night. These kids are sending Santa a letter, telling him what they want for Christmas."

"And how do you know that?"

"I've eavesdropped a time or two on the family where I grew up. My little friend, Cindy, she always writes a letter to Santa every year and she always seems to get what she wants."

"Interesting. But I don't get how this Santa drops the gifts from the sky."

"Well, actually he lands his sled on the roof of each house and goes down the chimney where he leaves the gifts for all the children all over the world."

"Every boy and girl?" "

If they've been good. I think they have to be good to get the gifts."

"That's sure a lot of work for one guy. And to keep track of everyone, that would be impossible. And to know what they want."

"I've never seen Santa in the sky but I think I know where we can find him. Sometimes he's in Family Park a few streets over."

"How about we go there now?" Marko asked. "I think I've seen enough city stuff, and I'm getting a little tired of dodging trampling feet."

"I'm ready for the park too," Bella responded.

"Wait," Marko stopped and pointed to a window. "This one is different. It's a country scene. And, look, a baby in a bed of straw. There's shepherds and sheep, even a cow and donkeys. They're all watching the baby. But how does this fit into Christmas?"

"That's what I'd like to know."

"I think this is my favorite window. My very favorite," Marko said.

Suddenly a snarling Jack Russel Terrier, inches from Bella and Marko, lunged at them, pulling hard against his leash.

With squeals of surprise and fright, Bella and Marko scrambled through a crack in a doorstep.

"Whew, that was close," Bella exclaimed. "Thankfully, dogs are always on a leash in the city."

"You can say that again," Marko agreed. "Good to know. You won't find dogs on a leash in the country."

"That dog is a Jack Russel Terrier and he's one of the worst mouse enemies. They think it's their job to get rid of rodents like us."

"We've got some mean dogs in the country too."

"I think it's safe now," Bella said. "We'll make one last stop at the park and then head for home."

As they hoped, they found Santa in the park; a friendly and jolly-looking man sitting on a sled. His most distinguishing feature was his long white beard. He wore a bright red coat. The park was all very spectacular, the icicle lights dangling from the entry gate, and sparkling glitter everywhere. The snow had stopped falling and the night sky was clear.

"Those reindeer hitched up to the sleigh, if they were real, they'd be ready to take off into the sky at Santa's command; at least so they say," Bella said. "I've just never seen Santa with real reindeer. The one at the front with the red nose, that's Rudolf. He's as famous as Santa in people land. See that big sack filled with stuff... those are gifts for the children."

"We know Christmas has a lot to do with gifts," Marko said. "The people on the streets were carrying lots of parcels. It seems like everyone is on a buying spree. And Santa Claus gives gifts to 'good' little boys and girls."

Reindeer - flickr/visualhunt/CC
Santa - visual hunt/CC

"Oh yes, everyone must buy each other gifts and they share them with each other on Christmas morning. It's all a big affair. Then they play games and have a big fancy meal together, the fixings are something to risk your life for."

"I think I've seen enough. We can go back to your place now."

The trek back to 33406 Walnut Lane was much less stressful than the trek into town. The shops had closed for the night, leaving only a coffee shop or two for the late nighters.

Traffic was quiet and the busses were asleep for the night. The snow was falling softly once again.

When they arrived at 33406 Walnut Lane, Bella suggested, "I want you to see something. We're going to peek into the Waxmann's living room window."

"I think they have the best-decorated home in all of Abbyville. It's so comfortable and warm inside, and not busy-looking at all. If Christmas were like this, I would be happy to have Christmas all the time."

The two tired mice climbed up to the Waxmann's window ledge. Marko had to agree with Bella regarding the Waxmann's living room.

"It looks like the Waxmann's grandchildren have come to visit," Bella said. Two children were sitting by the Christmas tree.

"I wonder what they're up to..."

"They're playing with something that's … the baby in the straw!" Marko said.

"Just like the baby in my favorite window."

"They are! We simply have to go inside. Maybe we can find out more about this baby in the straw. I know a way in. The mail slot in the front door; we can climb through it."

"I've done it before." Bella ran over to the door and jumped up to the brass object attached to it. "See, this will get us in. But we have to be careful no one sees us. Mrs. Waxmann is frightfully afraid of me."

"That's to our advantage then, I would think," Marko said as he jumped up and hung onto the brass bar alongside her.

In seconds they were inside the Waxmann's home and looking for cover. Their first stop, a crease in a sheepskin throw near the fireplace.

"I see a perfect place to hide," Bella whispered. She scurried over to the Christmas tree and scrambled up the side of a comfy chair with a dark-green sports coat draped over the arm.

She slipped into the pocket; Marko followed.

"Right. Perfect," Marko agreed. "No one will notice us here and we can listen in on what those two are saying."

"I can hear you," a playful voice said.

Busted! Bella and Marko froze...

A friendly looking freckled-face girl, with golden locks and bright blue eyes was looking right at them.

How had she noticed them? They had been ever so quiet, ever so careful...

"It's OK. We don't bite. We like mice, don't we Amy?"

Amy agreed.

"I'm Sabrina, and this is my little sister, Amy." The child's precocious smile matched the twinkle in her eyes.

"That's good to know—that you don't bite," Marko ventured.

"Yes, that is very good to know," Bella echoed. "We... I'm Bella and this is my friend Marko. I live just out back by the woodshed. My friend here is from the country, a long ways away. He came to the city to learn about Christmas. So this evening I took him to Christmas in the city. We've had a most exhilarating time and learned a lot."

"I don't think I've ever had so much exhilaration in one evening," Marko added. "By the time we got back I was quite happy to be off those busy streets. Exhilarating, but exhausting all at the same time."

"Mr. and Mrs. Waxmann's house is so inviting and I simply had to show Marko the most beautiful home in the city. That's why we climbed up to the window ledge where we could get a good peek inside."

"When we saw you and your sister with this baby in the straw—well, you see, it's just like the baby in the straw we saw in a store window display. And that was our favorite window," Marko said.

"We're curious how this baby fits into Christmas."

"Oh, Amy, we get to tell the story of the baby. We'd love to tell you the story of baby in the straw, wouldn't we, Amy?"

Amy agreed.

"But, you have to sit close to me. You don't want to miss a word."

Bella and Marko did not hesitate. They climbed down from their pocket-perch and nestled in close to Sabrina and the manger.

"The baby's name is Jesus and he's the savior of the whole world," Amy said.

"That's right, and this is his story..."

Sabrina began...

"Once upon a time, a long, long time ago there was a dark-haired, handsome man named Joseph and a sweet and beautiful-as-a-princess girl named Mary. They were engaged to be married. The thing was Mary was pregnant and the baby was not Joseph's."

"Oh, that could be a problem," Bella said.

"But this was a special child. You see, Mary was the baby's mother but God's spirit was his father. The baby was human but he was also God. God called this child His only Son."

"Why would God send his only son to earth as a baby?" Bella asked.

"To save people from all their sickness and sadness and badness."

"Oh. That's a big job."

"At this time, the ruler of the Roman empire, Caesar Augustus, decided everyone in the entire Roman world had to be counted."

"Everyone had to go to the town in which they were born to register. Joseph and Mary had to go to Bethlehem, a few days travel from where they lived."

"But there was a problem with traveling so far. Mary's baby was going to be born any day now. Joseph walked and Mary rode on their donkey. It was a long, tiring trip."

"Sure enough when they got to Bethlehem, the baby decided he wanted to be born right then. Joseph went from inn to inn, door to door trying to find a place with a bed for Mary."

"But every place was full. All the hotel rooms were full. Finally a kind innkeeper told them they could stay in his stable. Mary and Joseph were so thankful. That night Mary's special baby boy was born. She wrapped him in cloth they called swaddling clothes, and she laid him on a bedding of straw in a manger."

"What's a manger," Bella asked.

"It's a trough for cows to eat from," Marko the country mouse answered.

Sabrina continued, "Mary said, 'His name is Jesus because he is the savior of the world,' and because an angel told her that's what God said his name would be."

"Jesus," Bella said. "What a beautiful name."

Sabrina's voice became quiet and mysterious, "That same night, some shepherds were watching their sheep in the fields. Everything was still. The night sky was full of millions of twinkling stars. Some of the shepherds were sleeping by the fire."

When suddenly!...

"...something amazing happened. One of God's angels 'appeared to the shepherds and the glory of the Lord shone all around them.' The shepherds were terrified, as you can imagine."

Waiting For The Word on VisualHunt.com / CC BY

"But then the angel spoke and said, 'Do not be afraid. I bring you good news that will bring great joy for all the people, in the whole world. Today in the town of David (Bethlehem) a Savior has been born to you and he is the Messiah, the Lord. This will be a sign to you: you will find a baby wrapped in cloths and lying in a manger.'"

55

"Suddenly a great many heavenly angels appeared with the angel, all praising God and saying, 'Glory to God in the highest and on earth peace good will to men.'"

Sabrina recited the Bible verses perfectly, for you see, she had played the part of the angel in the Christmas pageant at her church the night before, and she knew the story of Jesus' birth by heart.

"Then everything was quiet and dark again," Sabrina continued. "The angels disappeared as suddenly as they appeared."

"When the Shepherds finally found their voices, they talked excitedly amongst themselves. 'Let's go to Bethlehem and see this thing that has happened which the Lord has told us about.' So they gathered their sheep and hurried to Bethlehem."

Sabrina knew everybody else's lines perfectly too, because one day she wanted to be an actress and because she loved the story of Jesus.

"The shepherds found Mary and Joseph and the baby Jesus, lying in the manger, just like the angel said. They worshiped him. Then they went and told everybody they could find, about this child, Jesus."

"I love this story," Bella said.

"There's more. I haven't told you about the wise men. One day, some wise men, who were kings, saw a bright star shining in the sky. As wise men, they knew something special was happening. They studied their scrolls and discovered a baby king, very important and sent by God, was going to be born soon. The wise men didn't waste a minute. They packed their bags, got on their camels, and followed the star."

"They stopped in Jerusalem, the capital of Israel. The wise men checked in with King Herod to ask him if he knew where this new king had been born. King Herod did not know either, so he asked HIS wise men and they checked their scrolls."

"They discovered a special king, a king of the Jews, would be born in the little town of Bethlehem, the City of David. King Herod told the wise men to go and find the baby, and then to come back and report. Herod said he wanted to worship the baby as well."

"That was a lie, wasn't it Sabrina," Amy interjected.

"It was a big lie. King Herod was evil and jealous. He planned to kill Jesus!..."

"Thankfully, the wise men had a dream where an angel told them not to go back to Herod but to go home another way."

"The star led the wise men right to Mary and Joseph and special baby Jesus."

"They brought him expensive gifts," Amy added. "Gold, and frankincenses and myrrh. Those are very expensive perfumes; cost lots and lots of money."

"Kings came to worship this baby," Marko said. "I think the kings are called wise men because they knew this baby was the King of Kings."

"Now you know how Christmas came to be," Sabrina said.

"Christmas is all about baby Jesus. He was born to bring peace to our hearts and to save us from our sins. Christmas is like a birthday party for Jesus, to remind us of what God did for us."

59

"So that's where this 'peace on earth, good will towards men' comes from," Marko said. "But how does Jesus save? How can a baby born so long ago, save people today?"

"Jesus had a very special mission. When he grew up, he was always healing people and helping them. But he was killed by the same people he came to save. He died a very sad way. They nailed him to a cross."

"Oh, that's so sad," Bella said. And Marko agreed. Everyone was somber for a moment.

"God said sin and bad things people do need to be paid for. So God sent his son Jesus to pay the price for everyone's sin. Everyone who has ever been born. He paid the price for all the bad things done and he did this so that we can all be forgiven for whatever bad things we've done and be acceptable to God."

"There's a devil in this world and he's a bad spirit. He tries to get people to follow him and do bad things. God is bigger and stronger than him and God proved it when He sent Jesus. Everyone can chose to serve Jesus and do good things, and not serve the devil."

"Wow. Now I know why I had to come and find out about Christmas."

"There's more," Amy said. "Jesus didn't stay dead. Tell them, Sabrina."

"He didn't?" Marko and Bella exclaimed in unison.

"Three days later Jesus came alive again. He rose from the dead, the Bible says. Jesus proved He was stronger and more powerful than death and any devil. God, who made everyone and everything, even little creatures like yourself, He thinks about us all the time. He loved His world so much He took care of evil and sent Jesus."

"So, all this other stuff about Christmas. All the busyness, I guess people sometimes forget the true meaning of Christmas. They give each other gifts, and that's good because we all like gifts, but sometimes they forget the best gift of all. Jesus. They forget He came to bring them peace, not busyness," Marko said.

"The celebrating and merry part of Chrismas all makes sense now," Bella said. "We have to celebrate something as great as this."

"Listen. I hear singing?" Marko interrupted.

"Carolers!" Sabrina and Amy shouted as they raced to the window. "They've come to sing to us. Come, come. Listen. They're singing 'Away in a Manger.'"

"Away in a manger, no crib for a bed
The little Lord Jesus laid down his sweet head..."

And Marko got his wish to hear carolers sing.

Several songs later, the carolers moved on down the street where they serenaded a family of seven.

Bella invited Marko to stay at her habitat for a few more days, until Christmas was over. Marko gladly accepted.

They talked long into the night hours while drinking hot chocolate and munching on walnut-date cookies by a warm, crackling fire.

Christmas day was all very grand, even grander than Marko could have imagined. Sabrina and Amy invited Marko and Bella to join them for the day. The girls gave them a Christmas experience they would never forget. Marko had never had so much to eat and never had things that tasted quite that good.

The time came for Marko to return to his home in the country. "I best be on my way. My family will be wondering if I'm OK." Marko chuckled.

"I can't wait to tell them all about you, Bella, and Christmas, and all our adventures."

During his stay at Walnut Lane, he and Bella had made several successful cheese runs and so he was able to keep his cheese promise to his friends.

The most important part of his adventure was that Marko brought Christmas to his country-mouse village. Ever since that day, the country mice celebrate Christmas and they all sit around a cozy fire and tell the story of the baby in the straw.

Marko's journey to find Christmas broadened his horizons far beyond any mouse's expectations.

His peers call him the **Traveling Warrior**.

Marko makes regular trips to Abbyville, sometimes even twice a month. On occasion he takes a brave and curious mouse or two with him.

Sometimes Marko makes the journey on his own. He is very thankful for his guardian mouse-angels.

He always makes a pitstop to spend time with his buddy, Brutus.

And Bella, she's waiting for him when he arrives at 33406 Walnut Lane.

About the Author

Carrie's interest in the arts began as a young girl. An imaginative child, she loved to draw, read, write and listen to stories. Their three-room school library consisted of a mere three short shelves of books, not nearly enough to satisfy her need for creative reading and storytelling.

After school Carrie would often run home to sit down beside their old-fashioned, console radio and listen to Aunt Ollie; a half-hour program where Aunt Ollie read fables, mysteries and other delightful tales.

Carrie's passion for storytelling and desire to create continued after marriage and children. She took several writing courses as well as pursuing painting, drawing and filmmaking.

Her love and passion for Jesus is evident in all her artistic endeavors. She writes for adults and children, fantasy and adventure being her favorite.

Carrie has a M.Min (Professional Writer) and D.Min (Fine Arts and Media).

Newfies to the Rescue - Tales of the Newfoundland Dog
Chuzzle's Incredible Journey - co-authored (daughter Minde Wagner)
The Ryder, 1991, 2nd. ed. 2015 - A Children's Fantasy Adventure
Treasure Trap - a sequel to *The Ryder*
Roadblocks to Hell - fiction based on a true story (adult)
Kickstart to a Healthier You - body, soul & spirit

Published by

HeartBeat Productions Inc.

Box 633, Abbotsford, BC, Canada V2T 6Z8

email: info@heartbeat1.com

tel: 604.852.3769

Made in the USA
Columbia, SC
10 December 2022